Tom Taylor, Henry L. Hinton

Tom Taylor's Drama of The fool's Revenge

Vol. 1

Tom Taylor, Henry L. Hinton

Tom Taylor's Drama of The fool's Revenge
Vol. 1

ISBN/EAN: 9783337334437

Printed in Europe, USA, Canada, Australia, Japan

Cover: Foto ©Andreas Hilbeck / pixelio.de

More available books at **www.hansebooks.com**

TOM TAYLOR'S

DRAMA OF

THE FOOL'S REVENGE

AS PRODUCED BY

EDWIN BOOTH.

Adapted from the Text of the Author's Edition, with Introductory Remarks, &c.,

By HENRY L. HINTON.

———————

NEW YORK:

PUBLISHED BY HURD & HOUGHTON,

459 BROOME STREET.

INTRODUCTION.

Tom Taylor, whose name is familiar to the modern play-goer, as the writer of many successful works, is the author of *The Fool's Revenge*. His claims to originality in the composition of this drama have been much questioned, but we shall let the author (or compiler) make his own defense. The following is his preface to the first edition of the play :—

'This drama is in no sense a *translation*, and ought not, I think, in fairness, to be called even an *adaptation* of Victor Hugo's fine play, '*Le Roi's Amuse.*'

'It originated in a request made to me by one of our most popular actors, to turn the libretto of Rigoletto into a play, as he wished to act the part of the jester. On looking at Victor Hugo's drama, with this object, I found so much in it that seemed to me inadmissible on our stage—so much, besides, that was wanting in dramatic motive and cohesion, and—I say it in all humility—so much that was defective in that central secret of stage effect, climax, that I determined to take the situation of the jester and his daughter, and to recast in my own way the incidents in which their story was invested.

'The death of Galeotto Manfredi at the hands of his wife Francesca Bentivoglio is historical. It seemed to me that the atmosphere of a petty Italian Court of the Fifteenth Century was well suited, as a medium for presenting the jester's wrongs, his rooted purpose of revenge, and the miscarriage of that purpose.

'I should not have thought it necessary to say thus much, had not some of the newspaper critics talked of my work as a simple translation of Victor Hugo's drama, while others described it, more contemptuously, as a mere *rifaciamento* of Verdi's libretto.

'Those who will take the trouble to compare my work with either of its alleged originals, will see that my play is neither translation nor *rifacia-mento.*

'The motives of Bertuccio, the machinery by which his revenge is diverted from its intended channel, and the action in the court subsequent to the carrying off of his daughter, are my own, and I conceive that these features give me the fullest right to call the *Fool's Revenge* a *new* play, even if the use of Victor Hugo's *Triboulet and Blanche* disentitle it to the epithet "*original*"—which is matter of opinion.

'For the admirable manner in which the drama is mounted and repre-sented at Sadler's Wells, and for the peculiarly powerful impersonation of Bertuccio, I owe all gratitude to Mr. Phelps. I must extend that feeling also to Miss Heath, Miss Atkinson, and the rest of the Sadler's Wells Company engaged in the representation of the *Fool's Revenge.*'

At the original presentation of this play at Sadler's Wells, London (1859), the piece was finely put upon the stage, but the period of action illustrated was one of about fifty years later date than the historical epoch, which the play actually presents, that of the murder of Galeotto Manfredi (1488). The piece was very creditably mounted at Niblo's Garden a few years since, when Mr. Edwin Booth personated the jester, and Miss Ada Clifton, Miss Rose Eytinge, and Miss Mary Wells, contributed to the completeness of the cast.

The present adaptation varies but slightly from the author's copy, one transposition being made, and a few lines omitted. The punctuation and the stage directions have been made in unison with the other plays of this series, a few superfluous directions having, however, been omitted.

COSTUME.

Cæsar Vecellio, who, in 1598, published in Venice a work on costume entitled *Habiti Antichi et Moderni*, gives in volume first, plate seventy-nine, a style of costume for women, well suited to this play, and one which was very general throughout all Italy at the period of its action. 'They wore,' he tells us, 'the *balzo* (a rounded head-dress) of various colors, and composed of a tissue of gold or of silk, and worked with a representation of flowers or other designs. They also carried gold chains, girdles of great value, and a fan with a highly ornamented holder. The shoulders were covered with a sort of plaited collar or neckerchief (bavero) of linen or cambric. The gown was generally of damask, of a crimson or violet color, having a lower border, six inches in width. The sleeves were slashed and puffed, permitting the chemise to come through. The cuffs, in which the arms of the chemise ended, accorded in style with the collar. The bodice, when worn, consisted of tissue of gold, and exceeded the ordinary length. Sometimes the robe was made so long as to trail on the ground.' The male attire at this time accorded with the female; indeed, in some of its details it did not differ at all. Vecellio, who has illustrated it (vol. I. plate 77), says :—'The men also wore on their heads a *balzo* similar to that of the women, made of leather, and round like a diadem; above this they placed a head-dress composed of a tissue of gold or silk. The shirt had a plaited bosom and a low ruffled collar. The waist of the coat was short, and the skirt reached to the knees; the sleeves were full, and extended to the elbow; the shirt-sleeves, which were provided with ruffled cuffs, covered the rest of the arm. The coat was ornamented with broad colored bands, made of cloth of gold or velvet or other material, according to the means of the wearer. The shoes were of velvet, and resembled those of the Germans.' The breeches, which are fastened below the knee, were slashed and puffed, and the shoes which were treated in a like manner were very broad at the toes. Vecellio gives (vol. I. plate 71) a graver style of dress, peculiar to this time, which was sometimes worn over the attire above mentioned. It is well suited to the more dignified personages of the drama, consisting as it does, of an ample garment, such as is known on the stage by the name of 'arm-hole-cloak.' This is made of silk or velvet, with a broad turn-over collar, sometimes of fur, and extends to the ancles; it is, however, furnished with hanging sleeves which may be worn at pleasure, over those of the under dress. The costume of the jester, it is scarcely necessary to say, should be of the motley order. Bertuccio is a domestic fool. He holds very much the same position under the duke Manfredi, as Touchstone does under the duke Frederick. 'The dress of Touchstone,' Mr. Douce remarks, 'should be a party-colored garment. He should occasionally carry a bauble in his hand, and wear ape's ears to his hood, which is probably the head-dress intended by Shakespeare, there being no allusion whatever to a cock's head or comb.'

DRAMATIS PERSONÆ

Of this adaptation of *The Fool's Revenge* as cast for its first representation at Booth's Theatre, New York, ——————.

GALEOTTO MANFREDI, lord of Faenza.........................——————

GUIDO MALATESTA, an old condottiere ....——————

BALDASSARE TORELLI,
GIAN MARIA ORDELAFFI, } nobles. { ....——————
.......................——————

BERNARDO ASCOLTI, a Florentine envoy ....——————

BERTUCCIO, a jester ....——————

SERAFINO DELL' AQUILA, a poet and improvisatore..............——————

ASCANIO, a page ....——————

GINEVRA, wife to Malatesta.................................——————

FRANCESCA BENTIVOGLIO, wife to Manfredi....................——————

FIORDELISA, daughter to Bertuccio ....——————

BRIGITTA, servant to Bertuccio ....——————

Chamberlains, Attendants, Servants, &c.

SCENE: *Faenza, and the Suburbs.*

FOOL'S REVENGE.

ACT I.

SCENE I. *A Loggia opening on the Gardens of Manfredi's Palace in the suburbs of Faenza. Moonlight. The gardens and loggia illuminated for a feast. Music at a distance.*

NOBLES *and* LADIES *moving through the gardens and loggia. Enter* ASCOLTI, *to* TORELLI *and* ORDELAFFI *discovered.*

Tor. Messer Bernardo, you shall judge between us,
Is Ordelaffi's here, a feasting face?
I say, 'tis fitter for a funeral.
　Asc. An Ordelaffi scarce can love the feast
That greets Octavian Riario,
Lord of Forlì and Imola.
　Ord. Because our line were masters there of old,
Till they were fools enough to get pulled down!
I was born to no lordship but my sword.
Thanks to my stout black bands, I look to win
New titles, and so grieve not over lost ones.
My glove upon't! I'll prove a lighter dancer,
A lustier wooer, and a deeper drinker,
Than e'er a landed lordling of you all.
Is it a wager?

MANFREDI *and* GINEVRA *pass by,* MALATESTA *appears
watching them.*

Tor. My hand to that! There's Malatesta's wife,
The fair Ginevra. Let's try lucks with her?
Asc. Ware hawk! Grey Guido's an old-fashioned husband;
Look how he glares upon the Lord Manfredi,
Each of his soft words to the fair Ginevra's
A dagger in the old fool's heart.
Ord. Sublime! ripe sixty wedded to sixteen,
And thinks to shut the foxes from his grapes!
Tor. The duke, too, for his rival! Poor old man!
Asc. Let the duke look to it. Ginevra's smiles
May breed him worse foes than Count Malatesta.
[*Whispering*] The duchess!
Tor. Faith, 'tis ill rousing Bentivoglio blood.
Ord. And she's as jealous as her own pet greyhound.
Tor. And sharper in the teeth. I wonder much
She leaves Faenza, knowing her Manfredi
So general a lover.
Asc. She leaves Faenza?
Tor.   So they say: to-morrow
Rides to Bologna to her grim old father,
Giovanni Bentivoglio.
Asc.   To complain
Of her hot-blooded husband?
Tor.   Nay, I know not:
Enough, she goes, and—fair dame as she is—
A murrain go with her, say I. There never
Was good time in Faenza, since she came
To spoil sport with her jealousy. Manfredi
Will be himself again, when she is hence.
Asc. Hush! here she comes—
Ord.   With that misshapen imp
Bertuccio. Gibing devil! I shall thrust

My dagger down his throat, one of these days!

Tor. Call him a jester? he laughs vitriol.

Asc. Spares nothing; cracks his random scurril quips
Upon my master, great Lorenzo's self.

Ord. Do the knave justice, he's a king of tongue-fence;
Not a weak joint in all our armours round,
But he knows, and can hit. Confound.the rogue!
I'm blistered still from a word-basting he
Gave me but yesterday. Would we were quits!

Tor. Wait! I've a rod in pickle that shall flay
The tough hide off his hump. A rare revenge!

Asc. They're here: avoid!

[*Ascolti, Ordelaffi, and Torelli mingle with the Guests.*

Enter FRANCESCA, *and* BERTUCCIO, *followed by two* Attendants.

Fran. [*Looking off, as if watching, and to herself*] Still with her!
   changing hot palms and long looks!
Her's for the dance, her's at the feast, all her's!
Nothing for me but shallow courtesies,
And hollow coin of compliment that leaves
The craving heart as empty as a beggar
Bemocked with counters!

Ber. [*Counting on his fingers and looking at the moon*] Moon—
   Manfredi—moon!

Fran. Ha, knave!

Ber.   By your leave, Monna Cecca,[1] I am cyphering.

Fran. Some fool's sum?

Ber.   Yes; running your husband's changes
Against the moon's. Manfredi has it hollow.
It comes out ten new loves 'gainst five new moons!

Fran. Where do I stand?

Ber. First of the ten; your moon was a whole honey one;
Excluding that, it's nine loves to four moons.

[1] 'Monna,'—Dame, Mistress; diminutive for Madonna. 'Cecca,'—Diminutive
for Francesca.

   1*

Fran. You pity me, Bertuccio ?

Ber.   Not a whit ;
I pity sparrows, but not sparrow-hawks.

Fran. I read your riddle,—I am strong enough
To right my own wrongs.   So I am, while here.

Ber. Then stay !

Fran.   My father at Bologna looks for me.

Ber. Then go !

Fran.   And leave him here—with her—both free,
And not a friend that I can trust to watch
And give me due report how things go 'twixt them.
Had I one friend—   .

Ber.   You have Bertuccio.

Fran. Men call you faithless, bitter, loving wrong
For wrong's sake, Duke Manfredi's worst councillor,
Still prompting him to evil.   .

Ber.   How folks flatter !

Fran. How, then, am I to trust you ?

Ber.   Monna Cecca,
You know the wild beasts that your husband keeps
Down in the castle fosse ?   There 's a she-leopard
I lie and gaze at by the hour together ;
So sleek, so graceful and so dangerous !
I long to see her let loose on a man.
Trust me to draw the bolt, and loose my leopard.

Fran. I 'll trust your love of mischief, not of me.

Ber. That 's safest !

Fran.   I must know how fares this fancy
Of Duke Manfredi for yon pale Ginevra :
Mark him and her, their meetings, communings ;
I know your 're private with my lord.

Ber.   He trusts me !

Fran. Here ! take my ring : your letters sealed with this,
My page Ascanio will bring me straight ;
'Tis but three hours' hard riding—and in six

I 'm here again.   Mark ! write not on suspicion,
Let evil thought ripen to evil act ;
That in the full flush of their guilty joys
I may strike sudden and strike home.
No Bentivoglio pardons.
 Ber.   Have a care !
Faenza is Manfredi's.   These court-flies,   [*Pointing to the Guests.*
Who flutter in the sunshine of his favour,
Have stings : the pudding-headed citizens
Love his free ways : he leaves their wives alone—
You play your own head, touching his.
 Fran. Give me my vengeance.   Then come what come may.
Enough ; I am resolved.   Now for the dance !
They shall not see a cloud upon my brow,
Though my heart ache and burn.   I can smile too,
On him and her.   Bertuccio, remember !
     [*Exit Francesca, followed by her Attendants.*
 Ber. [*Looking at the ring*] A blood-stone—apt reminder ! Does
    she think
That none but she have wrongs ?   That none but she
Mean to revenge them ?   What ? ' No Bentivoglio
Pardons.'   There is a certain vile Bertuccio,
A twisted, withered, hunch-backed, court buffoon,
A thing to make mirth, and to be made mirth of,
A something betwixt ape and man, that claims
To run in couples with your ladyship.
You hunt Manfredi, I hunt Malatesta,
Let's try which of the two has sharper fangs !

   MANFREDI *and* GINEVRA *re-appear in the background.*
The duke and Malatesta's wife !   [*Retires.*
 [*Manfredi and Ginevra come forward, Malatesta watching them.*
 Man. Not yet ! but one more round ! The feast is blank
For me when you are gone.   The flowers lack perfume,
Missing your fragrant breath.   The music sounds

Harsh and untunable, when your sweet voice
Makes no more under-melody.   O, stay !
   Gin. I am summoned, sir ; my husband waits for me.
   Man. What spoil-sports are these husbands [*Aside*] and these
       ·   wives !
Per Bacco !   I could wish Count Malatesta
Would lend my duchess escort to Bologna,
So we were both well rid.   [*Malatesta beckons to Ginevra.*
   Gin.   Your pardon, sir,
My husband beckons.   It is I, not you,
Must bear his moods to-night.   I dare not stay.
   Man. I would not bring a cloud to your fair brow
For all Faenza.   Fare you well, sweet lady !
                [*He leads her to Malatesta.*
I render up your jewel, Malatesta ;
See that you guard it as befits its price.
   Mal. Trust me for that, my lord.
   Man.   [*To Ginevra*] Sweet dreams wait on you.
   Mal. [*Aside*] This night sees her safe past Faenza's walls ;
She 's too fair for this liquorish court of ours.
             [*Exeunt Malatesta and Ginevra.*
   Man. A peerless lady !
   Ber.   [*Coming forward*] And a churlish spouse !
   Man. Bertuccio !
   Ber.   ' At your elbow, sir,' quoth Satanus.
   Man. Come, fool, let 's rail at husbands.
   Ber.   Shall I call
Your wife to help us ?
   Man.   Out on thee, screech-owl !
Just when I felt my chains about to fall
Thou mind'st me of my jailor.   Thank the saints,
I shall be free to-morrow, for awhile ;
I 'm thirsty to employ my liberty.
Come, my familiar, help me to some mischief ;
Some pleasant deviltry, with just the spice

Of sin to make the enjoyment exquisite.

Ber. Let's see, throat-cutting's pleasant, but that's stale ;
Plotting has savour in it, but 'tis too tedious ;
Say, a campaign with Ordelaffi's band,
So you may feed all the seven sins at once.

Man. Out, barren hound ! thy wits are growing dull.

Ber. A man can't always be finding out new sins ;
Think, they're as hard to hit on as new pleasures.
My head on't, Alexander had not run
So wide a round of pleasures, as you of sins ;
And yet he offered kingdoms for a new one.
You must invoke Asmodeus, not Beelzebub.

Man. What's he ?

Ber.   The devil specially charged with love ;
He has more work than all the infernal legion.
There's Malatesta's wife ; she's young, and fair,
And good, they say ; rare matter for sin there,
Though 'tis the oldest of them all.

Man.   But show me
How to win her ! She's cold as she is fair ;
I have spent enough sweet speech to have softened stone,
And all in vain.

Ber.   The monks say Hannibal
Melted the rocks with vinegar, not sugar.

Man. But she is adamant !

Ber.   When all else fails
You've still force to fall back on. Carry her off
From under Guido's grizzled beard.

Man.   By Bacchus,
There's mettle in thy counsel, knave ! I'll think on 't.

Ber. It needs no brains neither ; only strong hands
And hard hearts. Here come both.

Enter TORELLI, ASCOLTI *and* ORDELAFFI.

Man. What say you, gentlemen ; may I trust your arms ?

Tor. They 're yours in any quarrel.

Asc.   So are mine !

Ord.   And mine!

Ber. One at a time. You said ' arms'; of Torelli
You should ask legs ; his did such famous service
In carrying him out of danger at Sarzana,
I think they may be trusted.   [*All laugh except Torelli.*

Tor.   Scurril knave,
But I 'll be even with thee.

Ber.   That were pity.
A hump would be a sore disfigurement
Upon a back that you 're so fond of showing !

Asc. This rogue needs gagging.

Ber.   What, for speaking truth ?
I cry you mercy, I forgot how ugly
It must sound to a Florentine Ambassador.

Man. Well thrust, Bertuccio !

Ord.   My lord, my lord !
The slave is paid to find us wit—

Ber.   Hold there.
No man is bound to impossibilities,
'Tis a known maxim of the Roman law ;
How then can I find wit for Ordelaffi ? [*All laugh but Ordelaffi.*
But look, there 's Serafino, big with a sonnet:
I must help him to reason for his rhymes—

Man. Stay !

Ber.   Not I ! You 're for finding out new sins ;
With three such councillors, I am superfluous.
[*Aside*] The evil seed is sown ; 'twill grow, 'twill grow. [*Exit.*

Tor. Toad !

Asc.   Foul-mouthed scoffer !

Ord.   Warped in wit and limb !

Asc. My lord, you give your monkey too much rope,
He 'll soon forget all tricks in the scurvy one
Of making his grinders meet in our soft parts.

Man. Nay, give the devil his due ; if he hits hard,
He hits impartially.   I take my share
Of buffets with the rest.   Best cure the smart
By laughing at your neighbour that smarts worse ;
But about this business, where your arms may help me.
    Asc. Is it an enemy to be silenced ?
    Ord.   A castle
To be surprised ?   A merchant to be squeezed ?
    Asc. Or aught in which ducats or brains of Florence
Can help ?
    Man.   No.   Who was queen of the feast to-night ?
In your skilled judgement, Messer Gian Maria ?
    Ord. I ought to say your duchess, fair Francesca ;
But, if another tongue had asked the question —
    Man. Speak out thy honest judgement !
    Ord.   Not a lady
In all Faenza's worthy to compare
With proud Ginevra Malatesta !
    Tor. I think I know a fairer,—but no matter !
    Man. I hold with Ordelaffi.   I have mounted
Ginevra's colours in my cap, and heart ;
But she 's too proud, or fearful of old Guido,
To smile upon my suit.   'Tis the first time
I 've found so coy a dame.
    Asc.   Trust one who knows them,
The coyest are not always chastest.
    Man. How say you, if I spared her shame of yielding
By a night escalade ?
    Ord.   [*Shaking his head*] Carry her off ?
A Malatesta ?   Were it an enemy's town —
    Man. Hear him ! how modestly he talks !   Why, man,
Since when shrank'st thou from climbing balconies,
And forcing doors without an invitation ?
    Ord. O, citizens', I grant you ; but a noble's,
One of ourselves—

Asc.   Remember, Malatesta
Is cousin to the old Lord of Ceséna :
The affair might breed a feud, and so let in
The sly Venetian.
Tor.   Be advised, my lord ;
If you must breathe your new-fledged liberty,
Try safer game.   Old Malatesta's horns
Might prove too sharp for pastime.
Man.   Out, you faint hearts,
Do you fall off ?   Then, by Saint Francis' bones,
I and Bertuccio will adventure it.
Tor. Bertuccio !   My jewel to his hump,
'Twas he put this mad frolic in your head.
Man. And if it were ?   At least he'll stand by me.
Perchance his wits may be worth all your brawn.
Asc. Here comes one who may claim to be consulted
Upon this business.

Enter MALATESTA.

Man.   Guido Malatesta !
Why, how now, count ?   You left our feast so soon,
I thought you warm i' the sheets this good half-hour.
Mal. I had forgot my duty to your lordship;
So now repair my lack of courtesy :
To-morrow I purpose riding to Ceséna,
And would not go without due leave-taking.
Man. [*Aside*] This jumps well with my project.   What, to-
                    morrow !
You ride alone ?
Mal.   No, with my wife.
Man.   [*Aside*] The devil !
Why, this is sudden ; she spoke no word of this
To-night.
Mal.   Tush ! women know not their own minds,
How should they know their husbands' ?

Man.   But your reason?

Mal. Your air here in Faenza is too warm,
And scarce so pure as fits my wife's complexion ;
She 'll be better in my castle at Ceséna ;
The walls are five feet thick, and from the platform
There 's a rare view.   She 'll need no exercise.

Man. [*Aside*] The gaoler! [*Aloud*] But what says the lady's will?

Mal. I never ask that ; and so 'scape all risk
Of finding it run counter to my own.

Man. Faenza will have great miss of you both.

Mal. O, fear not, I 'll return ; your wine 's too good
To be left lightly.   I 'll be back to-morrow,
Before the gates are shut.   Meanwhile accept
This leave-taking by proxy from my wife.

Man. Not so ; I must exchange farewell with her
To-morrow.

Mal.   We shall start an hour ere dawn;
You 'll scarce be stirring.

Man.   [*Aside*] Plague upon the churl!
He meets me at all points.   At least, I hope,
This absence of your wife will not be long;
My duchess cannot spare her.   [*Aside*] Saints forgive me!

Mal. When your fair lady wants her, she can send :
I 'll answer for her coming on that summons.
Good night, sweet lords.   [*Aside*] How crest-fallen he looks !
Mass ! 'tis ill cozening an old condottiere !
Did he think I had forgot to guard my baggage?   [*Exit.*

Man. A murrain go with him !   May the horse stumble
That carries him, and break his old bull-neck !
O, this is cruel ; with my hand stretched out,
To have to draw 't back empty.   I could curse !

Tor. What if I helped you to a substitute
For coy Ginevra ? passing her in beauty :
One, too, whose conquest puts no crown to risk,
And helps withal a notable requital

That we all owe Bertuccio, you included.

Man. What mean you?

Tor.   Guess what's happened to Bertuccio.

Ord. He's grown good-natured.

Asc.   Or has dropp'd his hump.

Man. He has found a monkey uglier than himself.

Tor. No, something stranger than all these would be,
If they had happened. He has found a mistress! [*All laugh.*

Man. My lady's pet baboon? Bertuccio
Graced with a mistress!   [*He laughs.*

Asc.   She is blind, of course?

Ord. And has a hump, I hope, to match his own?

Man. Bertuccio with a mistress! why the rogue
Ne'er yet made joke so monstrous, or so pleasant. [*All laugh.*

Tor. Laugh as you please, sirs; on my knightly faith,
He has a mistress, and a rare one too.
Nay, if you doubt my word—Here comes Dell' Aquila,
He knows as well as I.

Man.   We'll question him.

Enter SERAFINO DELL' AQUILA.

Man. Good even to my poet—you walk late!

Aqu. [*Pointing to the moon*] I tend my mistress: poets and
          lunatics,
You know, are her liege subjects.

Man.   They are happy.

Aqu. Why?

Man.   They have a new mistress every month.
But jesters can find mistresses, it seems,
As well as poets. There's Torelli swears
Bertuccio has one, and that you know it.

Aqu. I know he has a rare maid close mewed up,
But whether wife or daughter—

Man.   Tell not me!
A mistress for a thousand! But what of her?

How did you find her out ?

Aqu.   'Twas some weeks since,
Attending vespers in your house's chapel,
At San Costanza, I beheld a maiden
Kneeling before that picture of our lady,
By Fra Filippo,— O, so fair, so rapt
In her pure passionate prayers,—I tell you, sirs,
I was nigh going on my knees beside her,
And asking for an interest in her orisons :
Such eyes of softest blue, crowned with such wreaths
Of glossy chestnut hair, a cheek of snow
Flushed tenderly, as when the sunlight strikes
Upon an evening alp, and over all,
A grace of maiden modesty that lay
More still and snowy round her than the folds
Of her white veil.   And when she rose I rose
And followed her like one drawn by a charm
To a mean house, where entering, she was lost.

   Man. She was alone ?

   Aqu.   Only a shrewish servant
That saw her to the church, and saw her home.

   Man. A most weak wolf-dog for so choice a lamb !

   Aqu. Methought, my lord, she needed no more guard
Than the innocence that sat, dove-like, in her eyes,
That shaped the folding of her delicate hands,
And timed the movement of her gentle feet.

   Man. You spoke to her ?

   Aqu.   I dared not ; some strange shame
Put weight upon my tongue.   I only watched her,
And sometimes heard her sing.   That was enough.

   Man. Poets are easy satisfied.   Well, you watched ?

   Aqu. And then I found that I was not alone
Upon my nightly post : there were two more ;
One staid outside, like me, and one went in.

   Tor. True to the letter !   I was the outsider,

The third, and luckiest, was Bertuccio!

Man. The hump-backed hypocrite!

Ord.   The owl that screeched
The loudest against women!

Asc.   But, is 't certain
That 'twas Bertuccio?

Tor.   I can swear to that.

Aqu. And I.

Asc.   How do you know him?

Tor.   By his hump,
His gait; who could mistake that crab-like walk?
I could have knocked my head against the wall
To think I had been fool enough to trust
A woman's looks for once. Dell' Aquila,
I know, holds other faith about the sex.

Aqu. I would stake life upon her purity;
Yet, 'tis past doubt Bertuccio is the man,
The ugly gaoler of this prisoned bird.

Man. Why that 's enough to make it a mere duty
To break her prison-house, and shift her keeping
To fitter hands,—say mine. I 'm lord of the town,
None else has right of prison here, but I.

Aqu. What would you do?

Man.   First see if she bears out
Your picture, Serafino; if she do,
Be sure I will not wait outside to mark
Her shadow. Shadows may suit poets; I
Want substance.

Tor.   She is for Bertuccio's master,
Not for Bertuccio. When shall it be?

Man.   To-morrow.
I 'm a free man! Meet me at midnight, here.

Aqu. You would not harm her? Only see her face,
You will not have the heart to do her wrong.

Man. What call you 'wrong'? To save so choice a creature,

From such a guardian as Bertuccio ?
He would have prompted me to play the robber
Of Malatesta's pearl : let him guard his own.

Ord. If he resists, we'll knock him o'er the sconce ;
Let me have that part of the business.

Man. Nay, I 'ld not have the rascal harmed ; he's bitter,
But shrewdly witty, and he makes me laugh.
No, spare me my buffoon : who does him harm,
Shall answer it to me.

Tor. 'Twere a rare plot to make the knave believe
Our scheme still held against old Malatesta :
That his Ginevra was the game we followed.

Ord. So give him a rendezvous a mile away ;
And, while he waits our coming, to break open
The mew where he keeps close his tercel gentle.

Asc. [*Aside to Manfredi*] Ne'er trust a poet. What if he betray us ?

Man. He's truth itself ; and where he gives his faith,
'T is better than a bond of your Lorenzo's.

Asc. Swear him to secrecy.

Man.   [*To Dell' Aquila*] Your hand upon it.
You'll not spoil our sport, by breaking to Bertuccio
What we intend ?

Aqu.   But think, O, think, my lord,
What if this were no mistress ; as, if looks
Have privilege to reveal the soul, she is none ?

Man. Mistress or maid, man, I will not be baulked ;
'Tis for her good. I know the sex ; she pines
In her captivity : I'll find a cage
More fitting such a bird as you've described.
Your hand on 't : not a whisper to Bertuccio !

Aqu. You force me ! There's my hand, I will not speak
A word to him !

Man. [*Taking his hand*] That's like a trusty liegeman
Of blind Lord Cupid ? [*To the others*] Hark, a word with you !

Aqu. I 'll save her from this wrong, or lose myself.
What tie there is betwixt these two I know not;
How one so fair and seeming gentle 's linked
With one so foul and bitter,—a buffoon,
Who makes his vile office viler still,
By prompting to the evil that he mocks.
But I will 'gage my life that she is pure.
And still shall be so, if my aid avail!   [*Exit.*

Man. But how to get sight of Bertuccio's jewel!
I 'ld see, before I 'ld seize.

Tor.   Trust me for that!
I am no poet: When I found the damsel
Admitted such a gallant as Bertuccio,
I thought it time to press my suit; and so
Accosted her on her way from San Costanza—

Man. She listened?

Tor.   Long enough—the little fool—
To learn my meaning; then she flushed, and fled;
I followed, when, as the foul fiend would have it,
Ginevra Malatesta coming by
From vespers with her train, sheltered the pigeon,
And spoiled my chase.

Man.   You did not give it up?

Tor. I changed my plan; the mistress being coy,
I spread my net to catch the maid.   O lord!
The veriest Gorgon!   You might swear none e'er
Had given her chase before!   no coyness there;
A small expense of oaths and coin sufficed
To make her think herself a misprized Venus,
And me the most discriminating wooer
In all Faenza.   'Twill not need much art
For me to win an entrance to the house,
And when I 'm in, it shall go hard, my lord,
But I find means to get you access too.

Man. About it straight; at dusk to-morrow night

Be here, armed, masked and cloaked.
    Ord.   While poor Bertuccio
Awaits our coming near San Stefano!
A stone's throw from the casa Malatesta.
    Asc. He's here!   .
             Enter BERTUCCIO.
    Ber.   Not yet a-bed!
Since when were the fiend's eggs so hard to hatch?
I left a pleasant little germ of sin
Some half an hour since: it should be full-grown
By this time.   Is it?
    Man.   Winged, and hoofed, and tailed.
If proud Ginevra Malatesta sleep
To-morrow night beneath old Guido's roof,
Then call me a snow-water-blooded shaveling.
    Ber. Ha! 'Tis resolved then?
    Tor.   We have pledged our faith
To carry off the fairest in Faenza—
    Asc. Before the stroke of midnight.
    Ord.   'Twas my plan
To gather one by one to the place of action;
Lest, going in a troop, we might awake
Suspicion, and put Guido on his guard.
    Ber. A wise precaution, although it was yours.
I wronged you, gentlemen; I thought you shrunk
Even from sin, when there was danger in't.
It seems there are deeds black enough to make
Even Torelli brave, Ascolti prompt
And Ordelaffi witty.   But the place?
    Man. Beside San Stefano.
    Ber.   The hour of meeting?
    Man. Half an hour after vespers.   There await us.
And now, good rest, my lords; the night wanes fast,
My duchess will be weary.   *[All laugh.*
    All.   *[Going]* Sir, good night!

Ber. Sleep well, Torelli.   Dream of charging home
In the van of some fierce fight.
Tor.   My common dream.
Ber. 'Tis natural; dreams go by contraries.
And you, Ascolti, dream of telling truth ;
And, Ordelaffi, that you have grown wise.
Tor. And, you, that your back's straight, your legs a match,
Asc. And your tongue tipped with honey.
Ord.   Come, my lords,
Leave him to spit his venom at the moon,
As they say toads do !   [*Exeunt all but Bertuccio, laughing.*
Ber.   Take my curse among you,
Fair, false, big, brainless, outside shows of men ;
For once your gibes and jeers fall pointless from me.
My great revenge is nigh, and drowns all sense :
I am straight, and fair, and well-shaped as yourselves ;
Vengeance swells out my veins, and lifts my head,
And makes me terrible !   Come, sweet to-morrow,
And put my enemy's heart into my hand,
That I may gnaw it !   [*Exit.*

ACT II.

Scene I.   *Faenza.   A room in Bertuccio's house.   The walls hung
with tapestry concealing a small recess and a secret door communicating with the street; a window opening on the street with a balcony; a statue of the Madonna in a recess with a small lamp
burning before it; a missal on a stand before the statue; a lute
and flowers; a lamp lighted.*

TORELLI *and* BRIGITTA *discovered.*

Bri. Hark, there's the quarter! you must hence, fair signor.
Tor. But a few moments more of your sweet presence ?

Bri. Saint Ursula, she knows, 'tis not my will
That drives you hence ; but if my master found
That I received a man into the house,
'Twere pity of my place, if not my life.

Tor. Your master is a churl, that would condemn
These maiden blooms to wither on the tree.

Bri. Churl you may call him ! why he 'ld have the house
A prison. If you heard the coil he keeps
Of bolts, and bars and locks ! Lord knows the twitter
I 've been in all to-day about the key
I lost this morning ; it unlocks the door
Of the turnpike stair that leads down to the street.

Tor. 'Twas lucky I came by just when you dropt it.

Bri. Dropt ! nay, signor, 'twas whipped off by some cut-purse,
That thought to filch my coin.

Tor.   That 's a shrewd guess !
He must have flung it from him where I found it,
Not knowing of what jewel it unlocked
The casket !

Bri. How can I pay your pains that brought it back !

Tor. By ever and anon giving me leave
To come and sun myself in your chaste presence.

Bri. Alas, sweet signor !

Tor.   O ! divine Brigitta !

Bri. But I must say farewell. Vespers are over ;
My mistress will be waiting, she 's so fearful.

Tor. As if her unripe beauties were in danger,
While your maturer loveliness can walk
The streets unguarded.

Bri. Nay, I 'm a poor, fond, thing ; Lord knows the risk
I run to let you in.

Tor.   I warrant now
You 've some snug nook where, if your master came,
You could bestow me at a pinch.

Bri.   I know none,

2

Unless 'twere here, [*Lifting arras from the recess*] behind the
        arras, look !
Here's a hole too, whence you could peep to see
When the coast 's clear !
    Tor.   [*Aside*] There 's room enough for two.
Brigitta !
    Bri.   Signor !
    Tor.   How if this had served
For hiding others before me ?
    Bri.   I swear
By the eleven thousand virgins—
    Tor.   That 's
Too many by ten thousand and nine hundred
And ninety-nine ! Vouch but your virgin self,
And I am satisfied !
    Bri.   Alack, a-day !
To be suspected after all these years.
    Tor. Pardon a lover's jealousy ; this kiss
Shall wipe away the memory of my wrong.
[*Aside*] What will not loyalty drive a man to ?   There !
                                        [*Kisses her.*
    Bri. [*Aside*] He has the sweetest lips ! And now begone,
Sweet signor, if you love me.
    Tor.   'If,' Brigitta !
Banish me then to outer darkness straight !
Farewell, my full-blown rose! let others prize
The opening bud ; the ripe, rich flower for me !
    Bri. O, the saints, how he talks ! This way, sweet signor.
                            [*Taking a key from her girdle.*
The secret door; the key you found and brought me
Unlocks it.   [*Unlocking secret door.*
    Tor. [*Taking another from his girdle, aside*] Else, why did I
        filch it from you,
And have this, its twin brother, forged to-day.

Bri. [*Getting the lamp*] I'll light you out, and lock the door
        behind you,
'Safe bind, safe find.'
Tor.   Good night, sweet piece of woman,
I leave my heart in pledge. [*Aside*] Now for the duke.
[*Brigitta holds open the door and lights him down, then locks the door.*
Bri. He's gone, bless his sweet face! To think what risks
Men will run that are lovers, and indeed
Weak women too! Lord! if my master knew.
'Tis lucky San Costanza is hard by,
I should be fearful else. Faenza's full
Of gallants, and who knows what might befall
A poor young woman like myself, with nought
Except her innocence to be her safeguard!   [*Exit.*

As soon as she has closed the door, the secret door opens, and TORELLI
re-enters with MANFREDI.

Tor. This way, my lord, the dragon has departed.
Man. 'Tis time; I was aweary of my watch.
Tor. You were alone, at least. Think of my lot,
That had to make love to a tough old spinster.
I would we had changed parts. Why, good, my lord,
I had to kiss her. Faugh! when shall I get
The garlic from my beard? But here's the cage
That holds our bird. We must ensconce ourselves,
For they'll be here anon; vespers were over
Before we entered.
Man.   Thanks to your device
Of the forged key. Yet that was scarcely needed;
I've climbed more break-neck balconies than that
                                          ·   [*Pointing to winu*
Without a silken ladder. [*Looking about*] So, a lute,,
A missal, flowers! more tokens of a maid
Than of a mistress. Well, so much the better; ·

I long to see the girl.   Is she as fair
As Serafino painted ?
   Tor.   Faith, my lord,
She 's fair enough to justify more sonnets
Than e'er fat Petrarch pumped out for his Laura.
She is a paragon of blushing girlhood,
Full of temptation to the finger-tips.
I marvel at myself, that e'er I yielded
This amorous enterprise, even to you ;
But that my loyalty outbears my love.
   Man. I will requite your loyalty, fear not ;
But where shall we bestow ourselves ?
   Tor.   [*Lifting the arras from the recess*] In here ;
The old crone showed it me but now—there 's cover
And peeping-place sufficient.   Hark ! they come :
Stand close, my lord.   [*They retire behind the arras.*

Enter FIORDILISA *and* BRIGITTA.

   Bri.   And he was there to-night ?
   Fio. O yes !   He offered me the holy water
As I passed in.   I trembled so, Brigitta,
When our hands met, I fear he must have marked it,
But that he seemed almost as trembling, too,
As I was.
   Bri.   ' He '!   a brazen popinjay,
I 'll warrant me, for all his downcast looks !
I wonder how my master would endure
To hear of such audacious goings on !
   Fio. That makes me sad.   My father is so kind,
I cannot bear to have a secret from him.
Sometimes I feel as I would tell him all ;
But then, I think, perhaps he would forbid me
From going out to church ; and 'tis so dull
To be shut up here all the long bright day :
From morn till dark to mark the busy stir

Under the window, and the happy voices
Of holiday-makers, that go out and in
Just as they please.   Look at the birds, Brigitta!
Their wings are free, yet no harm comes to them ;
I 'm sure they 're innocent!   And then to hear
Sometimes the trumpets, as the knights ride by,
And tramp of armed men, sometimes a lute. [*A lute sounds within.*
Hark, 'tis his lute!   I know the air, how sweet!
My good Brigitta, would there be much harm
If I touched mine—only a little touch—
To tell him I am listening ?
   Bri.   Holy saints,
Was e'er such boldness!   I must have your lute
Locked up.   These girls! these girls!   Bar them from court,
And they 'll find matter in church ; keep them from speech,
And they 'll make cat-gut do the work of tongue !
Better be charged to keep a cat from cream,
Than a girl from gallants !
   Fio.   Nay but, good Brigitta,
This gentleman is none.
   Bri.   How do you know ?
   Fio. He never speaks to me, scarce looks, or if
He do, it is but to withdraw his gaze
As hastily as I do mine.   I 've seen him
Blush when our eyes met ; not like yon rude man,
Who pressed upon me with such words and looks,
As made me blush—you know the time—
When that kind lady, Countess Malatesta,
Scarce saved me from his boldness.
   Bri.   Tilly-vally !
There are more ways of bird-catching than one ;
He 's the best fowler, who least scares his quarry.
But I must go and see the supper toward.
Your father will be here anon.   [*Exit.*
   Fio.   Dear father !

Would he were here, that I might rest my head
Upon his breast, and have his arms about me;
For then I feel there's something I may love,
And not be chidden for it. [*Lute sounds*] Hark! again!
If I durst answer!
How sad he must be out there in the dark,
Not knowing if I mark his music.

      [*Takes her lute, then puts it away*] No!
My father would be angry: sad enough
To have one joy I may not share with him;
Yet there can be no harm in listening.
I thought to-night he would have spoken to me,
But then Brigitta came, and he fell back.
I'm glad he did not speak, and yet I'm sorry,
I should so like to hear his voice,—just once,—
He comes in my dreams, now, but he never speaks—
I'm sure 'tis soft and sweet! [*Listening*] His lute is hushed.
What, if I touched mine, now that he is gone?
I must not look out of the casement! Yes,
I'm sure he's gone! [*Takes her lute and sings.*]
 Man. [*Aside, lifting the arras*] She is worth ten Ginevras!
 Tor. [*Holding him back*] Not yet!
 Man.   Unhand me, I will speak to her!
 Tor. My lord! It is Bertuccio! In, quick!

   BERTUCCIO *appears at the door.*

  [*His dress is sober and his manner composed. He stands for
   a moment at the door fondly contemplating Fiorde-
   lisa; then stepping quietly forward—*
 Ber. My own!
 Fio. [*Turning suddenly and flinging herself into his arms—*
   My Father!
 Ber.   Closer, closer yet!
Let me feel those soft arms about my neck,
This dear cheek on my heart! No, do not stir,

It does me so much good!   I am so happy ;
These minutes are worth years.
 Fio.   My own dear father!
 Ber. Let me look at thee, darling.   Why, thou growest
More and more beautiful!   Thou 'rt happy here ?
Hast all that thou desirest, thy lute, thy flowers ?
She loves her poor old father ?   Blessings on thee,
I know thou dost, but tell me so.
 Fio.   I love you,
I love you very much!   I am so happy
When you are with me.   Why do you come so late,
And go so soon?   Why not stay always here ?
 Ber. Why not! why not!   O, if I could!   To live
Where there 's no mocking, and no being mocked,
No laughter, but what 's innocent; no mirth
That leaves an after-bitterness like gall.
 Fio. Now, you are sad!   There 's that black ugly cloud
Upon your brow ; you promised, the last time,
It never should come when we were together.
You know when you 're sad, I 'm sad too.
 Ber.   My bird!
I 'm selfish even with thee ; let dark thoughts come,
That thy sweet voice may chase them, as they say
The blessed church-bells drive the demons off.
 Fio. If I but knew the reason of your sadness,
Then I might comfort you ; but I know nothing,
Not even your name.
 Ber.   I 'ld have no name for thee,
But ' father.'
 Fio. In the convent, at Ceséna
Where I was rear'd, they used to call me orphan.
I thought I had no father, till you came.
And then they needed not to say I had one;
My own heart told me that.
 Ber.   I often think

I had done well to have left thee there, in the peace
Of that still cloister.   But it was too hard,
My empty heart so hungered for my child;
For those dear eyes that look no scorn for me,
That voice that speaks respect and tenderness,
Even for me.   My dove, my lily-flower,
My only stay in life.   O God! I thank thee
That thou hast left me this at least.   [*He weeps.*
    Fio.   Dear father!
You're crying now; you must not cry, you must not,
I cannot bear to see you cry.
    Ber.   Let be!
'Twere better than to see me laugh.
    Fio.   But wherefore?
You say you are so happy here, and yet
You never come but to weep bitter tears.
And I can but weep too, not knowing why.
Why are you sad?   O, tell me, tell me all!
    Ber. I cannot.   In this house I am thy father;
Out of it, what I am boots not to say;
Hated, perhaps; or envied; feared, I hope,
By many; scorned by more, and loved by none.
In this, one innocent corner of the world
I would but be to thee a father; something
August, and sacred.
    Fio.   And you are so, father.
    Ber. I love thee with a love strong as the hate
I bear for all but thee.   Come, sit beside me,
With thy pure hand in mine, and tell me still,
' I love you,' and ' I love you,' only that.
Smile on me—so !—thy smile is passing sweet!
Thy mother used to smile so once.   O God!
I cannot bear it.   Do not smile, it wakes
Memories that tear my heart-strings.   Do not look
So like thy mother, or I shall go mad !

Fio. O, tell me of my mother!
Ber.   No, no, no!
Fio. She 's dead?
Ber.   Yes.
Fio.   You were with her when she died?
Ber. No! leave the dead alone, talk of thyself—
Thy life here. Thou heed'st well my caution, girl,
Not to go out by day, nor show thyself
There, at the casement.
Fio.   Yes. Some day, I hope,
You will take me with you, but to see the town;
'Tis so hard to be shut up here, alone.
Ber. Thou hast not stirred abroad?
Fio.   Only to vespers;
You said I might do that with good Brigitta.
I never go forth, or come in alone.
Ber. That 's well. I grieve that thou should'st live so close.
But if thou knew'st what poison 's in the air,
What evil walks the streets, how innocence
Is a temptation, beauty but a bait
For desperate desires:—no man, I hope,
Has spoken to thee?
Fio.   Only one.
Ber.   Ha! who?
Fio. I know not; 'twas against my will.
Ber.   You gave
No answer?
Fio.   No; I fled.
Ber.   He followed you?
Fio. A gracious lady gave me kind protection,
And bade her train guard me safe home. O father,
If you had seen how good she was, how gently
She soothed my fears—for I was sore afraid—
I 'm sure you 'ld love her.
Ber.   Did you learn her name?
    2*

Fio. I asked it, first, to set it in my prayers,
And then, that you might pray for her.
    Ber. Her name? [*Aside*] I pray!
    Fio.   The Countess Malatesta.
    Ber. [*Aside*] Count Malatesta's wife protect my child!
You have not seen her since?
    Fio.   No; though she urged me
So hard to come to her; and asked my name;
And who my parents were; and where I lived.
    Ber. You did not tell her?
    Fio.   Who my parents were?
How could I, when I must not know myself?
    Ber. Patience, my darling; trust thy father's love,
That there is reason for this mystery!
The time may come when we may live in peace,
And walk together free, under free heaven;
But that cannot be here, nor now!
    Fio.   O, when,
When shall that time arrive?
    Ber.   When what I live **for**
Has been achieved.
    Fio.   What you live for?
    Ber.   Revenge!
    Fio. O do not look so, father!
    Ber.   Listen, girl,
You asked me of your mother; it is time
You should know why all questioning of her
Racks me to madness. Look upon me, child;
Misshapen as I am, there once was one,
Who seeing me despised, mocked, lonely, poor,
Loved me, I think, most for my misery:
Thy mother, like thee, just so pure, so sweet.
I was a public notary in Ceséna;
Our life was humble, but so happy: thou
Wert in thy cradle then, and many a night

Thy mother and I sate hand in hand together,
Watching thine innocent smiles, and building up
Long plans of joy to come.
  Fio.   Alas ! she died.
  Ber. Died ! There are deaths 'tis comfort to look back on:
Her's was not such a death.   A devil came
Across our quiet life, and marked her beauty,
And lusted for her ; and when she scorned his offers,
Because he was a noble, great and strong,
He bore her from my side, by force, and after
I never saw her more : they brought me news
That she was dead !
  Fio.   Ah me !
  Ber.   And I was mad,
For years and years, and when my wits came back—
If e'er they came—they brought one haunting purpose,
That since has shaped my life—to have revenge :
Revenge upon her wronger and his order ;
Revenge in kind ; to quit him, wife for wife !
  Fio. Father, 'tis not for me to question with you :
But think—revenge belongeth not to man,
It is God's attribute ; usurp it not !
  Ber. Preach abstinence to him that dies of hunger,
Tell the poor wretch who perishes of thirst,
There's danger in the cup his fingers clutch ;
But bid me not forswear revenge.   No word !
Thou know'st now, why I mew thee up so close ;
Keep thee out of the streets ; shut thee from eyes ,
And tongues of lawless men ; for in these day,
All men are lawless.   'Tis because I fear
To lose thee, as I lost thy mother.
  Fio.   Father,
I 'll pray for her.
  Ber. Do, and for me ; good night !
  Fio. O, not so soon ; with all these sad dark thoughts,

These bitter memories.   You need my love :
I 'll touch my lute for you, and sing to it.
Music, you know, chases all evil angels.

   Ber. I must go : 'tis grave business calls me hence.
[*Aside*] 'Tis time that I was at my post.   My own,
Sleep in thine innocence.   Good night ! good night !

   Fio. But let me see you to the outer door.

   Ber. Not a step further, then.   God guard this place,
That here my flower may grow, safe from the blight
Of look, or word impure, a holy thing
Consecrate to thy service, and my love !

[*Exit Bertuccio and Fiordelisa.—Manfredi and Torelli come forward.*

   Man. His daughter !   That so fair a branch should spring
From such a gnarled and misshapen stock !

   Tor. But did you mark how he raved of revenge
Upon our order ?

   Man.   By the mass, I think
That Guido Malatesta is the man
That played him the shrewd trick he told the girl of.
'Twas at Ceséna, marked you ; the time fits.
That 's why he hounds me on after the countess,
What ! must I be the tool of his revenge ?
I 'll teach the scurril slave to strike at nobles !

   Tor. Hark !   what 's that ?   [*Listening.*

   Man.   'Tis outside the window !

   Tor.   [*Listening.*] Yes,
By Bacchus, some one climbs the balcony !

   Man. A gallant ?

   Tor.   In, sir ; see the play played out.

   Man. But I 'll not be forestalled !

   Tor.   We 've time enough.

                      [*They retire to the recess.*

Enter AQUILA *from the balcony.*

   Aqu. Pardon, sweet saint, if I profane thy shrine.

I watched Bertuccio forth, he passed me close,
I feared he would have seen me.   I have sworn
Not to betray their foul design to him.
And to warn her, this means alone is left me.
Hark ! 'tis her gracious step ; she comes this way.

Enter FIORDELISA.

Fio. Comfort of the afflicted, comfort him !
Turn his revengeful purpose to submission,
And grant that I may grow to take the place
My mother has left empty in his heart !
He 's gone ! And I had not the heart to speak
Of the young gentleman who follows me.
He asked if any spoke to me ; I told
The truth : he never spoke to me.   [*Seeing Aquila.*
                            Who 's there ?
Brigitta !   help !
   Aqu.   Silence ! but have no fear ;
I am not here to harm you, do not tremble.
I would die, lady, rather than offend you.
   Fio. O sir, how came you here ?
   Aqu.   I knew no other way
But by the balcony.   Desperate occasions
Dispense with ceremony.   My respect
Is absolute.   Fear not : I am not here
To say ' I love you,' nor to tell you how
For months your face has been my beacon star.
My passion never would have found a tongue,
It is too reverent : but your safety, lady,
I can be bold for that.
   Fio.   My safety !
   Aqu.   Threatened
With desperate danger.   Think you one so fair
Could even pray in safety in Faenza ?
You have been seen : your beauty hath been buzzed

In the court's amorous ear : there is a projeét
To scale your balcony to-night.
 Fio.   O father !
 Aqu. He cannot save you ; what were his sole strength
Against the bravos that the duke commands,
For any deed of ill. My arm and sword
Are stronger than your father's, and are yours
As absolutely. And yet what were these ?
I could die for you, but I could not save you.
 Fio. What shall I do ?
 Aqu.   Have you no friends, proteétors
To whom you might betake yourself?
 Fio.   Alas !
I am a stranger here.
 Aqu.   Think, have you none ?
 Fio. Ha ! if the Countess Malatesta—
 Aqu.   What ?
You know her?
 Fio.   She once rescued me from insult
Of a rude man ; and promised help whene'er
I chose to seek it.
 Aqu.   She is good, and pure,
And powerful moreover—that 's the chief.
Go to her straight ; you have no time to lose.
Midnight is fixed for their foul enterprise.
 Fio. But how to find the house ? And then the streets
Are dark and dangerous. I 've but our servant,
Brigitta—
 Aqu. Not a word to her ! She 's false.
Can you trust me ? I 'll lead you to the countess.
 Fio. [*Aside*] Were this a stratagem !
 Aqu.   I see you doubt me,
I know you have good cause to doubt all men.
O, could I bare my heart, and show you there
Your image set amongst its holiest thoughts,

Beside my mother's well-remembered face :
Could truth speak with the tongue, look from the eyes,
You would not doubt me.   What can oaths avail ?
He who could cheat you, would not fear to cheat
God and his saints !   Lady, it is the truth
That I have spoken !   May heaven give you faith
To trust in me ; but if not, I will stay,
And die in your defence.
  Fio.   Sir, I will trust you,
And heaven so deal with you, as you with me.
Go with me to the Countess Malatesta,
I 'll seek the shelter of her roof to-night,
To-morrow must bring counsel for the future.
  Aqu. O, bless you for this trust ! Come, quick, but softly.
Put on your veil, fear not, I am your guard,
Your slave, your sentinel.   I crave no guerdon,
Not even a look !   Enough for me to save you.
      [*Exeunt Fiordelisa and Dell' Aquila.*
  Man. [*Breaking from behind the arras, Torelli following him.*
Why did you hold me back? Our project 's marred.
This moonstruck poet bears away the prize,
And I am fooled.
  Tor.   Nay ; trust my cooler brain.
I 'll follow him to Malatesta's.   Sure
He 'll give her shelter ?
  Man.   In his lady's absence ?
  Tor. Even so.   The old ruffian can be courteous
When there 's a pretty face in question !
  Man.   Let him !
I 'll break his house, or any man's that dares
Set his locks in the way of my good pleasure !
  Tor. Why not ?   'Twill give a double pungency
To our revenge upon Bertuccio.
We only looked to keep the foul-mouthed knave
Out of the way while we bore off his pearl ;

But now we'll use him for the robbery.
He shall see us scale Malatesta's windows ;
But she whom we bear thence, muffled and gagged,
Shall be the hunch-backed scoffer's pretty daughter.
   Man. A rare revenge ! and so this brain-sick poet
And my curst jester may console each other.
Watch them to Malatesta's ; I'll to our friends,
And find Bertuccio by San Stefano.   [*Exit by secret door.*

SCENE II. *The same. A street near the Church of San Stefano.*

Enter BERTUCCIO, *masked and cloaked.*

   Ber. The hour has struck, they will be here anon ;
Trust them to keep tryst for a villanous deed.
I had need to whet the memory of my wrong,
Or my girl's angel face, and innocent tongue
Had shaken even my steadfastness of purpose.
And Malatesta's wife has done her kindness :
I would that she had not !   But what's such slight service
To my huge wrong ?   Let me but think of that !
I grow too human near my child ; I lack
The sharp sting of court scorn to spur the sides
Of my intent.   With her I'm free to weep ;
With them, I still must laugh, still be their ape
To mop, and mow, and wake their shallow mirth.
True, I can sometimes bite, as monkeys do.
They'll make mirth of that too !   O, courtly sirs !
Sweet-spoken, stalwart gallants ! if you knew
The hate that rankles underneath my motley,
The scorn that barbs my wit, the bitterness
That grins behind my laughter, you would start,
And shudder o'er your cups, and cross yourselves
As if the devil were in your company.
Once my revenge achieved, I'll spurn my chain,

Fool it no more, but give what 's left of life
To thought of her I 've lost, and love of her
That yet is left me.

Enter MANFREDI, ASCOLTI *and* ORDELAFFI, *masked and cloaked.*

Man.   Hist, Bertuccio!
Ber. Here, gossip Galeotto ; you are punctual :
Ascolti too.   Grave Signor Florentine,
We 'll show you how the gallants of Faenza
Treat greybeards who aspire to handsome wives.
Remember your beard's grizzled, and beware.
  Asc. I will stand warned.   You have the ladders here?
  Ber. The lackeys wait in charge of them hard by.
But where 's Torelli? we shall want his help.
  Ord. Pshaw! our three swords are plenty.
  Ber.   Cry you mercy!
'Tis not Torelli's sword we want.
  Ord.   What then ?
  Ber. His marvellous quick scent of danger, man.
Stick to his skirts, I 'll answer for 't, you 're safe.
Perhaps he smelt some risk of buffets here
And so has ta'en him home to bed.
  Man.   Away
Towards Malatesta's house ; 'twas there he promised
To meet us.   Sirrah fool, be it thy post
To hold the ladder while we mount ; and see
Thou play'st us no jade's trick, or 'ware the whip!
  Ber. Fear not, magnanimous gossip; do your work
With as good will as I do mine.   The countess
Sleeps in the chamber of the balcony,
Which rounds the angle of the southern front ;
I came but now by the palace : all was quiet.
  Man. Set on then, cautiously : use not your swords
Unless on strong compulsion ; blood tells tales,
And I want no more feuds upon my hands.

SCENE III. *The same. Exterior of Malatesta's Palace. A window on the second floor, with a balcony.*

Enter FIORDELISA *and* DELL' AQUILA, *followed by* TORELLI *at a distance.*

Aqu. Be of good cheer, this is the house ; I 'll knock
And summon forth the count.   [*Knocks.*
Fio.   O sir! what thanks
Can e'er repay this kindness ?
Aqu.   But remember
Who 'twas that did it, I am thanked enough.
Fio. I 'll pray for you, after my father.   Hark !
Aqu. They come !

Enter a Servant *from house.*

                    Two strangers who crave instant speech
Of the Count Malatesta.   [*Exit Servant.*
Aqu. And should I see your father ?
Fio.   Then you know him ?
Aqu. Yes.
Fio.   And his business, occupations ?   [*He bows.*
'Tis more than I do, sir, that am his child.
I do not even know his name.
Aqu.   What he
Keeps secret from you 'tis not mine to tell ;
'Twere well you should not question him too closely :
He shall learn you are safe.
Fio.   And tell him, too,
That 'twas you saved me, sir.   Promise me that.

Enter MALATESTA.

Mal. Who is it would have speech of Malatesta ?
Aqu. You know me, count ?
Mal.   Dell' Aquila, well met ?
But your companion ? [*Aside*] Ha ! a petticoat !
So ho, my poet !

Aqu.   Pardon, if I pray
This lady's name may rest a secret, count ;
She is in grievous danger ; one from which
Your house can shelter her.   She owes already
Your countess much, for good help given at need,
So craves to increase the debt.
    Mal.   My house is hers,
But she should know my countess is not here.
    Fio. Not here !
    Mal.   But if she dare trust my grey hairs
She shall have shelter.
    Aqu.   Nay, she cannot choose.
    Mal. I 'll give her my wife's chamber, if she will ;
Her woman to attend her.
    Aqu.   All she needs
Is your roof's shelter for the night ; to-morrow
Must see her otherwise bestowed.
    Mal.   Go in
Fair lady ; my poor house, with all that 's in it
Is at your service.   Had my wife been here,
You had had gentler tendance ; as it is
I 'll lead you to her chamber, and there leave you.
    Tor. [*Aside*] Now to the hunters : I 've marked down the deer.
                                        [*Exit.*
    Mal. [*To Aquila*] You will not stay and crush a cup with me ?
    Aqu. No, not to-night.   [*To Fiordelisa*] Did you not well to
            trust me ?
Farewell ; think of me in your prayers.
    Fio.   I cannot
Choose but do that, sir.   [*Aside*] O, the thought of him
Will come, henceforth, betwixt my prayers and heaven !
                    [*Exit Malatesta, leading in Fiordelisa.*
    Aqu. His child !   Since when did grapes grow upon thistles ?
And yet I 'm glad to know the tie that binds
The two together such a holy one.

Sweet angel, sister angels guard thy sleep!
Now, to seek out Bertuccio, and tell him
The danger she has 'scaped, and thank the saints
That made me her preserver.   [*Exit.*

Enter BERTUCCIO, MANFREDI, ASCOLTI, ORDELAFFI, *and* TO-
RELLI, *with* Servants *carrying ladders.*

 Man. Softly, you knaves! With velvet tread, like tigers!
 Ber. Say rather, ' cats.'   [*A light appears at the window.*
 Tor.   Which is the balcony?
 Ber. That. I have noted in this summer weather
The window's left unbarred.
 Asc.   Ha, there's a light!
If she were stirring?
 Ber.   What, an' if she were?
A sudden spring—a cloak flung o'er her head—
If she have time to scream, you are but bunglers.
 Man. My cloak will serve.   [*Takes it off.*
 Asc.   If she alarm the house
It might go hard with us.
 Ber.   O cats that long
For fish, yet fear to wet your feet! I'll shame you.
Let me mount first. Give me your cloak, Galeotto!
 Man. By your leave, fool, I'll net my own bird. Back!
Hold thou the ladder; that is lacqueys' work,
And fits thee best. Ascolti and Torelli,
Guard the approaches! I and Ordelaffi
Will be enough to mount, and snare the game.
 [*The light is extinguished; the Servants set a ladder to the balcony.*
 Ber. [*Holds it*] All's dark now. Up!
 Man.   Why, rogue, how thy hand shakes!
Is't fear?
 Ber. 'Tis inward laughter, Galeotto.
To think how blank Guido will look to-morrow

To find the nest cold, and his mate borne off!
[*Manfredi mounts the ladder, followed by Ordelaffi ; they enter.*
Ber. [*Listening*] Ha! they are in by this time. Cautious fools!
I had done 't myself in half the space! So, Guido,
You love your young wife well, they say; that 's brave.

MANFREDI *and* ORDELAFFI *re-appear on the balcony, bearing* FIOR-
DELISA *in their arms, muffled in Manfredi's cloak; she struggles,*
but cannot scream; they come down the ladder.
Ber. 'Tis done!
Man.   Away all; to my garden house,
There to bestow our prize!
[*Exeunt all but Bertuccio, the Servants, carrying off the ladder.*
Ber.   Now, Malatesta,
Learn what it is to wake, and find her gone
That was the pride and joy of your dim eyes,
The comfort of your age. I welcome you
To the blank hearth, the hunger of the soul,
The long dark days, and miserable nights.
These you gave me; I give them back to you.
I, the despised, deformed, dishonoured jester,
Have reached up to your crown, and pulled it down,
And flung it in the mire as you flung mine.
Now, murdered innocent, thou art avenged!
I cannot sleep. I 'll walk the night away.
It is no night for me, my day has come.   [*The curtain falls.*

ACT III.

SCENE I. *Manfredi's Garden-house. A Room with folding doors*
at the back, communicating with an inner chamber, and side en-
trances, covered by curtains.

Enter FIORDELISA.

Fio. Where am I? What has happened? Let me think.

Those men—that blinding veil—the fresh night air,
That struck upon my face—then a wild struggle,
In strong and mastering arms—then a long blank.
I must have fainted ; when I woke I lay
On a rich couch in that room.   Has he brought me
Into the very danger that he said
· He came to take me from ?   O cruel !   No,
Falsehood could ne'er have found such words, such looks.
Father !   O, when he comes and finds me gone !
I must go hence !   [*Looking round*]   That door—[*She runs to side
          entrance*] 'tis locked ! [*Shaking door*] Help ! help !
How dare they draw their bolts on me ?   My father
Shall punish them for this !   I will go forth !
                    [*Shakes door again ; the door opens from within.*
At last !   Whoe'er you are, sir, help me hence !

Enter MANFREDI.

Take me back to my father !   He will bless you,
Reward you—
    Man.   Nay, your own lips must do that.
    Fio. O, they shall bless you too, sir.
    Man.   To be blessed
With that sweet mouth were well, yet scarce enough.
    Fio. O sir, we waste time.   Set what price you will
On the great service, I am sure my father
Will pay you.   [*Manfredi relocks the door.*
    Man.   If we 're to discuss your ransom
'Twere fairest we should do it with closed doors,
The terms can scarce be settled, till you know
Your prison—gaoler—in what risk you stand.
First, for your prison : know you where you are ?
    Fio. No.
    Man.   In the Duke Manfredi's palace.   Next :
Know you your gaoler ?
    Fio.   Who ?

Man.   Manfredi's self.

Fio. Woe 's me!

Man.   What? Is the news so terrible?

Fio. I 've heard Brigitta and my father, too,
Speak of the Duke Manfredi.

Man.   [*Aside*] Here's a chance
To hear a genuine judgement of myself!
They said—

Fio.   That he was cruel, bold, unsated
In thirst for evil pleasures; it was odds
Whether more feared, or hated, in Faenza.

Man. [*Aside*] Trust the crowd's garlic cheers, and greasy caps!
The knaves shall know me worse ere they have done.
I thank you, pretty one; I am the duke.

Fio. Then heaven have mercy on me!

Man.   If report
Speak truth, your prayer were idle; but report
Is a sad liar. Do I look the ogre
They painted to you? Nay, my fluttered dove,
Smooth but those ruffled feathers; look about you.
Is this so grim a dungeon? Was your couch
Last night so hard, your 'tendance so ungentle?
I am your prisoner, fairest, not you mine.

Fio. Then let me go.

Man.   Not till you know at least,
What you will lose by going. All Faenza
Is mine, and she I favour may command
Whate'er Faenza holds of wealth or pleasure;
I 'll pour them at her feet, and after fling
Myself there too, to woo a gracious word.
What 's life, ungraced by love? a dismal sky
Without sun, moon, or starlight! 'Tis a cup
Drained of the wine that reddened in its gold,
A lute shorn of its strings, a table stripped
Of all its festal meats, mere life in death.

,A jewel like thy beauty is not meet
To be shut in a chest ; it should be set
To shine in princely robes, to grace a crown.
I would set thee in mine.   [*Approaching her*
    Fio.   Stand back, my lord.
    Man. Why, little fool, I would not harm a hair
On thy fair head.   Think what thy life has been,
How dull, and dark, and dreary !   It shall be
As bright, and glad, and sunny, as the prime
Of summer flowers.   Only repel not joy
Because it comes borne in the hand of Love.
    Fio. O, you profane that name !   Is love the friend
Of night, and violence and robbery ?
Let me go hence, I say.   I have a father
Who 'll make you terribly abye this wrong,
Lord as you are !
    Man.   Your father !   By the mass,
She makes me laugh !   Your father, girl !   Bertuccio !
    Fio. That I should learn my father's name from him !
Yes, duke, my father !
    Man.   Why, he is my slave,
A thing that crouches to me like my hound,
To beg for food, or deprecate the lash,
My butt, my whipping-block, my fool in motley.
    Fio. It is not true.   This is a lie, like all
That you have said.   Let me go forth, I say.
    Man. You 're in my palace.   Here are none but those
To whom my will is law ; your calls for help
Will only bring more force—if I could stoop
To use force with a lady.
    Fio.   Then you have
Some manhood in you.   Look, sir, at us two :
You are a duke, you say ; your power but bounded
By your own will.   I am a poor weak girl,
E'en weaker than I knew, if what you say

Touching my father, be the truth.   What honour
Is to be won on me ?   Yet, won it may be,
By yielding to my prayers to be set free,
To be sent home.   O, let me but go hence,
As I came hither ;   I will speak to none
Of this night's outrage ;   even to my father.
   Man. Ask anything but this.
   Fio.   Nothing but this !
You have a wife, my lord; what if she knew ?
   Man. The more need to take care that you tell her not.
Come, little one, give up these swelling looks,
Though they become you mightily.   [*Approaching her.*
   Fio.   Stand off !
[*He pursues her, she flies*] Help ! help ! [*Running to the folding door.*
         A door ! ha ! [*She forces it open, and rushes in.*
   Man.   ·   [*Locking it outside*] Deeper in the toils !
[*Laughs*] The lamb seeks shelter in the wolf's own den !
   Tor. [*Outside*] My lord !
   Man.   [*Unlocks the door*] Torelli's voice ! how now, Torelli ?

Enter TORELLI.

   Tor. My lord, the duchess is returned.
   Man.   Why, man,
Thy news is stale ; the duchess has been here
These five hours ; she arrived, post haste, ere sunrise.
She must have ridden in the dark.   'Twas that
Prevented me from making earlier matins
Before my little saint here.
   Tor.   Do you know
What brought the duchess back so suddenly ?
   Man. Some jealous fancy pricked her, as I judge
From her accost when we encountered first ;
And, as I gathered, she suspects contrivance
Betwixt me and the Countess Malatesta.
'Twas a relief, for once, that I could twit her

3

With groundless fears. I told her Malatesta
Rode yesterday with his lady to Ceséna,
And, for more proof, repeated what he said,
That on my wife's least summons, she'ld return;
So she has summoned her, in hopes, no doubt,
To catch me in a lie. Her messenger
Rode to Ceséna, just at daybreak. Soon
We may look for him back, bringing, I hope,
Ginevra Malatesta.

    Tor.   This is rare.
So falls she off the scent, and leaves you here
To follow up your game with Fiordelisa.

    Man. Even so. I excused me from her presence
By work of state, for which to this pavilion
I had summoned you and the Envoy of Florence,
Said work of state being no less a one
Than to lend me your presence at the banquet
I mean to offer our fair prisoner.
Bid Ordelaffi and Ascolti hither,
And send my men with fruits and wines and sweetmeats,
All that is likeliest to tempt the sense
Of this scared bird.

    Tor.   How did you find her, sir?

    Man. Beating her pretty wings against the bars;
Still calling for her father. Shrewdly minded
To peck, instead of kissing, silly fledgling!
But I will tame her yet, till she shall come
To perch upon my finger.

    Tor.   Where is she?

    Man. In the inner room, whither she fled but now.
Fear not, I turned the key on her; she's safe.

    Tor. I'll send what you command, and warn the rest
That you attend them. Good speed to your wooing.   [*Exit.*

    Man. Now for my prisoner! By gentle means
To gain her ear. Asmodeus, tip my tongue

With love's persuasion !   [*Exit into inner room.*

Enter the DUCHESS FRANCESCA *masked, and* BERTUCCIO, *who has
resumed his fool's dress.*

Fra. [*Unmasking*] Was't not Torelli went hence, even now ?
Ber. I think it was.   Be sure he saw us not.
Fra. Then you still bear me out, my husband lies ?
That Malatesta's wife has not gone hence ?
Ber. Trust a fool's eyes before a husband's tongue.
I say again, I was at hand last night
When your lord bore from Malatesta's house
Said Malatesta's wife.   I saw the deed.
I heard the order given to bring her hither.
Fra. Then 'twas by force, not by the lady's will,
She came ?
Ber.   Force ?   Quotha—force !   How many ladies
Have had to bless the ' force ' that saved their tongue
An awkward ' yes.'   See you not what an answer
' Force ' finds for all ?   It stops a husband's mouth ;
Crams its fist down the town's throat ; nay ; at a pinch
Perks its sufficient self in a wife's face :
Commend me still to ' force.'   It saves more credits
Than e'er it ruined virtues.   After folly,
I hold force the best mask that wit has found
To mock the world with !
Fra.   There 's weight in that.
This violence would stand her in good stead,
Were she e'er called in question !   Then what matter,
        [*Bertuccio, who has been moving round the room, stops opposite
            folding doors.*
So I be wronged, if 'tis by force, or will.
Would I had certain proof !
Ber.   Ha !   You want proof ?
Come here ;   [*The Duchess approaches him.*
        Stand where I stand.   Now listen—close.

Fra. [*Listening at door*] My husband's voice in passionate en-
    treaty !

Ber. Only his voice ?

Fra.   An answering voice ! a woman's !
These are your state affairs, my gracious duke !

Ber. If you would have more proof, I'll bring you where
You shall hear his humble tools in last night's business
Discuss the deed ; all noble gentlemen,
Who 'ld pluck my hood about my ears if I
Durst hint a doubt of their veracity.

Fra. Do so, and if they bear thy story out
I know my part.

Ber.   What, tears ?

Fra.   Tears ?   Death to both.

Ber. Take care.   His guards are faithful.   Can you trust
A hand to do the deed ?

Fra.   I trust my own.

Ber. Women turn pale at blood.   Your heart may fail you,
When the time comes to strike.

Fra.   Daggers for men.
I know a surer weapon.

Ber.   [*Whispering*] Poison ?

Fra.   Hush !
The Borgia's physician gave it me !
It may be trusted !

Ber. [*Aside*] My she leopard's loosed at last !   [*Exit.*

Fra. [*Still at the door, listening.*]
Past doubt, a woman's tongue !   And now my husband's !
How well I know the soft, smooth, pleading voice ;
The voice that drew my young heart to my lips
When, at my father's court, I plighted troth
To him, and he to me.   O bitterness !
Now spurned for each new leman of the hour !
O, he shall learn how terrible is hate
That grows of love abused.   [*Taking a vial from her bosom.*

Come, bosom friend,
That hast lain cold, of late, against my heart,
As if to whisper to it, ' Be thou stone,
When the time calls for me.'   [*Looking at the vial.*
                    Each drop's a death.
What matter who she be?   Enough for me
That she usurps the place that should be mine
In Galeotto's love.   Hark! some one comes.
            [*She conceals the vial, and resumes her mask.*

Enter two Chamberlains *with white wands, followed by* Attendants
    bearing a banquet, and pass into the inner room. After them a
    Page *with wine in a golden flagon, goblets, fruit, &c., on a salver.*

[*Stopping the Page*] Hold, sir, set down your charge.
    Page.   By your leave, madam,
'Tis for my lord.
    Fra.   Since when was that an answer
To give thy lady?   [*Removes her mask.*
    Page. [*Aside*] 'Tis the duchess!   Pardon ;
I knew you not.
    Fra.   Enough, sir, set it down,
And wait without till I bid thee bear in.   [*Exit Page.*
What need of further proof?   Is 't heaven or hell
That sends this apt occasion?   Galeotto,
I warned thee in the spring-time of our loves,
This hand could kill as easy as caress ;
You laughed, and took it in your ampler palm,
And said that death were pleasant from such white
And taper fingers.   Try it now!
        [*She pours some of the contents of the vial into the flagons of wine.*
                    'Tis done!

Re-enter BERTUCCIO.

    Ber. Hide, here, Madonna : here their lordships come!
I met them on the way, so brave and merry.

My gossip Galeotto bids them here—
To feast with him and her !   [*Exit.*
  [*Francesca starts as if stung, then goes to the door and beckons.*

  Re-enter Page, *she signs to him, he bears in the wine.*

Fra.   [*Aside*] Their doom is sealed !
                          [*She retires behind curtains.*

  Re-enter BERTUCCIO, *with* ASCOLTI *and* ORDELAFFI.

Ber. It is your due ; you that go out bat-fowling
Lack wine o' mornings to keep up your hearts.
  Ord. Why thou wert there knave ; yet try thou to enter
Into the presence, and they 'll whip thee back ;
His highness wants no fool to-day !
  Ber.   That 's true,
With you two for his company.   But tell me,
How will the lady relish o'er her wine,
The cut-throat faces that she saw last night ?
Methinks 'twill mar her appetite.
  Asc.   Be sure
She will not look so scared at us,
As thou wouldst at the sight of her.
  Ber.   Who, I ?
Nay, I but held the ladder : we, poor knaves,
Must take the leavings of your rogueries,
As of your feasts.   But prithee, Ordelaffi,
How looked she ?
  Ord.   Wouldst believe it ?
Methought she had a something of thy favour ;
As, if so crook'd a thing could have a daughter,
Thy daughter might have had.   [*All laugh, Bertuccio starts.*
  Asc.   How now ! he winces.
There cannot, sure, be issue of thy blood !
Nature 's too merciful ; she broke the mould
When she turned thee out !

Ber.   Nature, sir, proportions
Her witty fools to her dull ones ; while she makes
Ascoltis, she must needs produce Bertuccios
To sting their hard hides now and then.   But tell me,
Think you Ginevra needed all that force ?

Ord. She struggled stoutly ; but a lady's struggles,
I take it, are much like her ' no,' which often
Must be read, ' yes.'

Asc.   Let 's in at once, my lords.

Ber. I 'll marshal you ; who said that cap and bells
Should be shut out ?

Asc.   Stand back, Sir Fool, 'twere best ;
You may repent your pressing on too far.

Ber. I fain would see the lady ; 'tis not often
That one can carry a beauty off at night,
And make her laugh i' the morning.

Ord.   Neither she,
Nor you, I think, are like to breed much mirth
Out of each other.

Ber.   Say you so ?   Here goes ! [*He runs up to the door—*

The Page *opens it and motions him back* ; *the two* Chamberlains
appearing at the open door.

Why, how now, sirrah ?   I 'm the fool !

Page.   Stand back !

Ber. I ! why I 'm free o' the palace ; every place
Except the council-chamber, and in that
I sit by proxy !

Page.   'Tis the duke's strict order
You enter not this room. [*Bertuccio is pressing forward.*] Back !
          or the grooms
Shall score thy hunch to motley.   [*He closes the door.*

Asc.   How now, sirrah,
Call you this marshalling ?

Ber.   I am right served !

I forgot that fools in silks should take precedence
Of fools in motley! Lead the way, my lords!

Ord. Look, here comes Malatesta.

Ber.   Ha! but stay
To hear me gird at him! You call me bitter;
Now you shall see how merciful I've been.

Asc. Waste not your ears on him, the duke awaits us
Beside his beauty—metal more attractive
Than this curst word-catcher.

Ord.   Aye, aye, let's in.

                          [*Exeunt Ordelaffi and Ascolti.*

Enter FRANCESCA.

Ber. Now, now, Madonna, have you proof enough?

Fra. Mountains of proof on proof, if proof were needed;
But had disproof come with them, and not proof,
'Tis all too late.

Ber.   How?

Fra.   I have drugged their wine.
They will sleep sound to-night.   [*She retires up stage.*

Ber.   [*Aside*] Choose woman's hands.
You that would have grim work nimbly despatched.
Here's Malatesta!—looking black as night.
So, lord, I hope you liked your waking news.
Now, now, to gloat over his agony!

Enter MALATESTA.

Mal. Ha, knaves! I'ld see the duchess.

Ber.   Marvellous!

Mal. How now?

Ber.   To think, that they can make such caps
To hide all trace of them.

Mal.   Of what, knave?

Ber.   Horns.

Mal. Rascal!

Ber.   I hope your lordship had good rest ;
And that my lady, too, slept undisturbed.
    Mal. What mean you, sirrah ?
    Ber.   Nay, strain not so hard
To keep it down ; you are among friends here.
A grievous loss, no doubt,—but at your age
You could scarce look to keep her to yourself.
Others have lost wives, too,—poor knaves who thought
To stick in their thrum-caps jewels that caught
The eyes of nobles ; needs were they must yield
Daughters—or wives.
    Mal.   Art mad, or drunk, or both ?
My errand's to thy mistress, not to thee.
Where is she ?
    Fra.   [*Coming forward*] Here, my lord ! [*They talk apart.*
    Ber. .   He bears it bravely.
But wounds will bleed under an iron corslet ;
And how his must be bleeding—for he loved her ;
The whole court vouches it.
                [*Francesca and Malatesta come forward.*
    Fra. You say your lady slept not here, last night,
But at Ceséna?
    Mal.   Or the devil's in't.
I saw her safe bestowed there : I can trust
My own eyes, or still better, my own bolts.
    Ber. [*Aside*] Is this old man, too, of Manfredi's council,
To cheat his wife ?
    Mal. I little thought to bring her back so soon ;
But, on your summons, I have straight recalled her.
    Ber. And she is here : hold him to that, Madonna.
    Mal. Malapert dog !
    Fra.   Pardon his licensed tongue.
I fain would see the lady.
    Mal.   You shall see her ;
I have not far to fetch her.   [*Exit*

Ber.   'Tis a lie!—
A cursed lie, to hide his own foul shame!
Believe him not!
  Fra.   But if he bring the lady?
  Ber. Aye, if he bring the lady, then believe him!
[*Aside*] He robs me of my right, taking his wrong
With outward show of calm. Mine turned my brain.
I looked to see him mad, or drive him so!
  Man. [*Within*] More wine, knave!

A Page *passes through for wine.*

  Fra. Ginevra, or another, what of that?
The wrong's the same, why not the same revenge?
  Ber. The same to you, but not the same to me!
I tell you Malatesta's wife sits yonder—
Sits at your husband's side. I saw her—I—
Borne off last night! I saw. There is no faith
In eyes or ears·or truth, if 'twere not she!

Re-enter MALATESTA, *with* GINEVRA. *Bertuccio's back is towards
the door.*

  Mal. Madam, my wife!
  Ber.   [*Turning*] Ginevra here! then who
Was that they carried from her bed last night?
Who is't sits yonder?
  Fra.   Tell me, gracious lady,
Where did you sleep last night?
  Gin.   Where I scarce thought
To leave so soon, your highness; in Ceséna,
Within my husband's castle.
  Fra.   Pardon, madam,
That I have set you on a hurried journey,
Still more that I have wronged you in my thoughts!
                              [*Laughter heard within.*
[*Aside*] They laugh! laugh on, my lord. while it is time.

Gin. Wilt please you grant me audience: you shall hear
To the minute how my hours went yesterday,
Down to this moment.
    Fra.   Come out in the air ;
I stifle within hearing of their mirth.
[*To Bertuccio*] Stay here! see that the other 'scape me not.
                                    [*Exeunt Francesca and Ginevra.*
    Ber. The other! Not Ginevra? [*To Malatesta*] Good, my lord,
Your wife slept at Ceséna, yet her chamber
Was not untenanted last night, I 'll swear!
    Mal. And so thou mightst, yet break no oath.
    Ber. Who slept in 't ?
    Mal. I know not. Ask Dell' Aquila : 'twas he
Brought me the lady, craving shelter for her
From some great danger.
    Ber.   But you saw her face ?
    Mal. And if I did, think'st thou I 'ld trust her name
To thy ass-ears ?   [*Exit.*
    Ber.   Fooled, mocked of my revenge!
The sweetest morsel on 't whipt from my teeth !
O, I could brain myself with my own bauble !

                Enter DELL' AQUILA.

[*Aside*] Dell' Aquila ! He knows.
    Aqu.   Well met, Bertuccio ;
I 've sought thee since this morning, nay, since midnight.
    Ber. Ha !
    Aqu.   For a matter much concerns thy peace.
Thou hast a daughter. [*Bertuccio starts.*] How I know thou hast
Matters not to my story.
    Ber.   Hush, hush, hush !
If you know this, as you are Christian man
And poet,—poets should have softer hearts
Than courts and camps breed now-a-days,—O keep
The knowledge to yourself !

Aqu.   It is too late
Torelli knew it; had set wolfish eyes
On her—
  Ber.   Well? well?
  Aqu.   Had rung her beauty's praise
Here in the court—thou hast no friends here—
  Ber.   Well?
  Aqu. They plotted how to lure thee from the house;
And in thy absence, to surprise her window,
And bear her off! They bound me by an oath
To keep it secret from thee, not from her.
I swore to save her, or to lose myself;
So I found a desperate means of speech with her,
And warned her of her danger.
  Ber.   Thanks, thanks, thanks,
But only warned her!
  Aqu.   Placed her too in safety.
  Ber. O heaven! where?
  Aqu.   In the house of Malatesta.
  Ber. My child in Malatesta's house last night!
  Aqu. Secure; even in the countess's own chamber.
  Ber. My child! My child!—wronged, murdered!
  Aqu.   Ha! by whom?
  Ber. By me, by me! Her father, her own father,
That would have grasped heaven's vengeance, and have drawn
The bolt on my own head—and her's—and her's!
  Aqu. What do you mean?
  Ber.   I counselled the undoing
Of Malatesta's wife; I stood and watched,
And laughed for joy, and held the ladder for them,
And all the while, 'twas my own innocent child.
Look not so scared, 'tis true!—I am not mad!
She's here—now—in their clutches!   [*Laughter within.*
                        Hark, they laugh!
'Tis the hyenas o'er their prey—my child!

And I stand here and cannot lift a hand!
Aqu. Here's mine, and my sword too!
Ber.   O, what were that
Against their felon blades?
Aqu.   True, true! what aid?
Ha! there's the duchess!
Ber.   I had forgotten her!
                [*Drawing Aquila to him and whispering.*
Man, she has drugged their wine, the bony Death
Plays cupbearer to them; if she drinks, she dies.

Enter a Page *with wine.*

Look, look. Perchance, that is the very wine.
                [*He assumes the Fool's manner.*
Halt there, for the fool's toll. No wine goes in
But pays the fool's toll.
Page.   Out, knave, stand aside!
          [*Bertuccio overthrows the flagon from the salver.*
Ber. 'Tis forfeit by the law!
Page.   Thy back shall bleed
To make it up. Now must I go fetch more,
And brook the cellarer's chiding for thy folly.

Enter TORELLI.

Ber. [*To Aquila*] If he goes in, could we but enter with him,
A word of mine might save her from the poison.   ·
                [*Gets between Torelli and the door.*
Tor. Good day, Sir Poet; stand aside, Sir Fool.
Ber. You are going in?
Tor.   Aye.
Ber.   There's a shrewd hiatus
Needs filling at the table. You have War
And Love, but lacking Poetry and Folly,
War is but butchery, and Love goes lame.
Tuck us beneath your wings, sweet Baldassare,

And you 'll be trebly welcome.

[*Seizing him by one arm; motions Dell' Aquila to take the other.*

Tor. The duke for once has shut his doors against
Both Poetry and Folly.   He is cloistered
For grave affairs.

. *Ber.*   Tush, tell me not, sweet gossip.
Why, man, I know that there 's a petticoat ;
And more, I know the wearer.

Tor.   Thou !

Ber.   You've lost
The rarest sport.   Ascolti and Ordelaffi
Have had their will of me.   For once I 'll own
You 've turned the tables fairly on the fool !
That our Ginevra should be Fiordelisa,
And poor Bertuccio not know !   Ha, ha !
O excellent !   It was a sleight of hand
I shall remember to my dying day.

Tor. Nay, an thou tak'st it so.

Ber.   How should I take it ?
Besides the pleasantness of it, there 's the honour.
Think, my poor daughter in the duke's high favour.
Why, there are counts by scores, had pawned their scutcheons
To come into such grace.   I warrant now,
You thought I 'ld swear, and storm, and rend you all,
So shut me out.   But, lo you, I am merry,
And so shall she be, if you 'll let me in !
But let me in, I 'll school the silly wench ;
Teach her what honour she has come to ; thank
The gracious duke, and play the merriest antics.
You 'll swear you never saw me in such fooling ;
But take me in.

Tor.   Why now ; the fool's grown wise !
I 'll tell the duke, perchance he 'll let thee in.   [*Exit.*

[*Bertuccio, exhausted by his emotions, falls into a chair, and writhes convulsively.*

Aqu. Lives hang on minutes here.   Said you the duchess
Had mixed the poison, or but meant to mix it ?
     Ber. There it is, man, I know not which.   Even now
Death may be busy at her lips.   Once in,
In my mad antics, I might spurn the board,
And spill the flagons as I did e'en now ;
But here I'm helpless.   O Bëelzebub !
Inspire them with desire to see a father
Make laughter of the undoing of his child !
Ha ! some one comes.   They 'll let me in !
     Tor.   [*At the door*] The duke
Will none of thy ape's tricks.
          [*He closes the door.   Bertuccio wrings his hands and screams.*
     Aqu.   What ho !   Torelli !
And you within, you, my lord duke, 'fore all,
I do proclaim you cowards, ruffians, beasts.
Come out, if you be men, and drive my challenge
Back in my throat, if you 've one heart among you !
     Ber. You speak to men ; they're fiends !
     Aqu.   No hope, no hope !
Yes ! here's the duchess, she's a woman still.

          Enter FRANCESCA, GINEVRA, *and* MALATESTA.

     Ber. Madam, and you, too ; [*To Ginevra*] plotting your un-
               doing,
I 've compassed the destruction of my child,
The daughter that I loved more than my life.
'Twas she they seized last night, and she's in there.
     All. Your child ?
     Ber. Look, Guido Malatesta, I am he
Whose wife, long years ago, you stole from him ;
I am Antonio Bordiga !
     Mal.   You ?
     Ber. I thirsted for revenge, for that I wrought
Upon the duke to carry off your wife ;

Your innocent Ginevra ; seeking that,
See to what verge of terrible disaster
I've brought my own dear daughter.
[*To Francesca*] From death, if not wrong worse than death,
You still may save her.   Have the doors burst open.
You can command here, next the duke.   If not,
At least [*Aside to her*] forbear the poison.
    Fra.   [*Aside to him*] 'Tis too late
The wine was here.
    Ber.   Then this alone remains.
                  [*He rushes up to the door and shouts.*
Come forth, my lords !   The duke's life, all your lives
Hang by a thread.   Come forth, all !   For your lives !

       Enter TORELLI, ASCOLTI, *and* ORDELAFFI.
Your wine is poisoned !
    Tor.   Ha !   Who did the deed?
    Ber. I !   drink not, for your lives !
          [*They are rushing upon him, drawing their swords.*
    Fra.   He lies ! .'Twas I !
                    [*A shriek within.*
    Ber. My child !   my child !
    Tor.   [*Who has turned back at the*
sound, flinging the door wide open]   Look to the duke, my lords !

MANFREDI *is seen senseless on his seat,* TORELLI, ASCOLTI, *and*
    ORDELAFFI *supporting him, and* FIORDELISA *lying at his feet.*

    [*Bertuccio and Dell'Aquila rush up to Fiordelisa. Malatesta
        and Ginevra exeunt.*
    Ber. Too late !   Too late !
    Tor.   He's dead !
    Fra.   Before all men,
I 'll answer this !
    Ber.   Before heaven's judgement-seat,
How shall I answer this ?   [*Pointing to Fiordelisa.*

*[Dell' Aquila has brought Fiordelisa forward.   Bertuccio takes
her in his arms.*

       Dead ! dead ! My bird—
My lily flower—gone to thy last account,
All sinless as thou wert ? My fool's revenge,
Ends but in this. Cold! cold ! *[Putting his hand on her heart.*
      Ha ! Yes ! a beat !
A breath ! A full deep breath ! She lives ! she lives !
Say some of you, ' She drank not,' and I 'll bless
The man that says so ; yea, so pray for him
As saints ne'er prayed ! She breathes—still. Hark ! hark !
 Fio. Father !
 Tor. She never drank ! Thou hast her pure as when
She kissed thy lips last night !
 Ber.   O, bless you, bless you ?
She lives, lives, lives ! Leave us to pray together.
 Tor. [*To Francesca*] Madam, you are our prisoner ; the duke
Lies foully murdered.
 Fra.   Ha ! what call you ' foully ?'
Who but myself can estimate my wrongs ?
For those who stand, like him, past reach of justice,
Vengeance takes Justice's sharp sword.
My father, Giovanni Bentivoglio
Stands at your gates, in arms ! Let who will, question
Francesca Bentivoglio of this deed !
 Fio. Father, let 's pray for her !
 Ber.   For her !—for me !
We need it both ! Ah, thou said'st well, my child ;
Vengeance is not man's attribute, but heaven's.
I have usurped it. Pray—oh, pray for me. [*The curtain falls.*